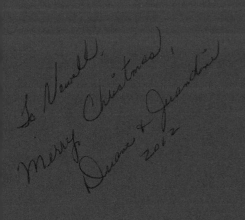

To Newell,
Merry Christmas!
Duane + Juandine
2012

86 YEARS

The Legend of the
BOSTON RED SOX

by Melinda R. Boroson

illustrated by Gary R. Phillips

Brown House
BOOKS

For information about permission to reproduce selections from this book, write to

Permissions, Brown House Books, 95 Sawyer Road, Suite 400, Waltham, MA 02453.

www.brownhousebooks.com

Book design by Kathryn K. Reynolds

ISBN 0-9767938-0-6

Printed in China

10 9 8 7 6 5 4

The publisher is donating a portion of the book's proceeds to the Jimmy Fund.

For my mother, Hannah,
who always believed
— M. R. B.

To the Game,
whose soul is team spirit
and humility
— G. R. P.

'Twas back in nineteen-eighteen, when great-grandpa was a boy,
When baseball filled his head with dreams and filled his heart with joy,
In Boston, folks would hurry down to Fenway Park to see
Their hometown team, the Red Sox, play the game triumphantly.

3

Four splendid times they'd led the league, with four World Series wins.
That year the Red Sox won a fifth! (Here's where the myth begins . . .)
The owner tried to clear some debts, if what they say's the truth,
And to the Yankees of New York he sold away Babe Ruth.

It seemed their luck was gone as soon as Babe was off the team,
And then the thrill of championship was nothing but a dream.
As years went by, the Red Sox fared no better, only worse,
'Til people started thinking that there had to be a curse.

And as for the World Series, well, the Red Sox just seemed stuck.
The Curse of the Bambino's what they called that rotten luck.
It seemed they'd never win, and sure enough, though they came near,
The Sox cleared out their lockers deep in sorrow every year.

6

That heartache wove through years and years, three generations long.
In '46 or '86, it played the same sad song.
So close! The team could glimpse the prize, right there beyond their reach,
But every chance would slip away, like waves along a beach.

Then came two-thousand-four; the Sox were in the Wild Card spot.
The challenge lay before them; every game would be hard-fought.
But, lo! a sweep of Anaheim! The Sox could still achieve!
And fans began to whisper, then to thunder, "We believe!"

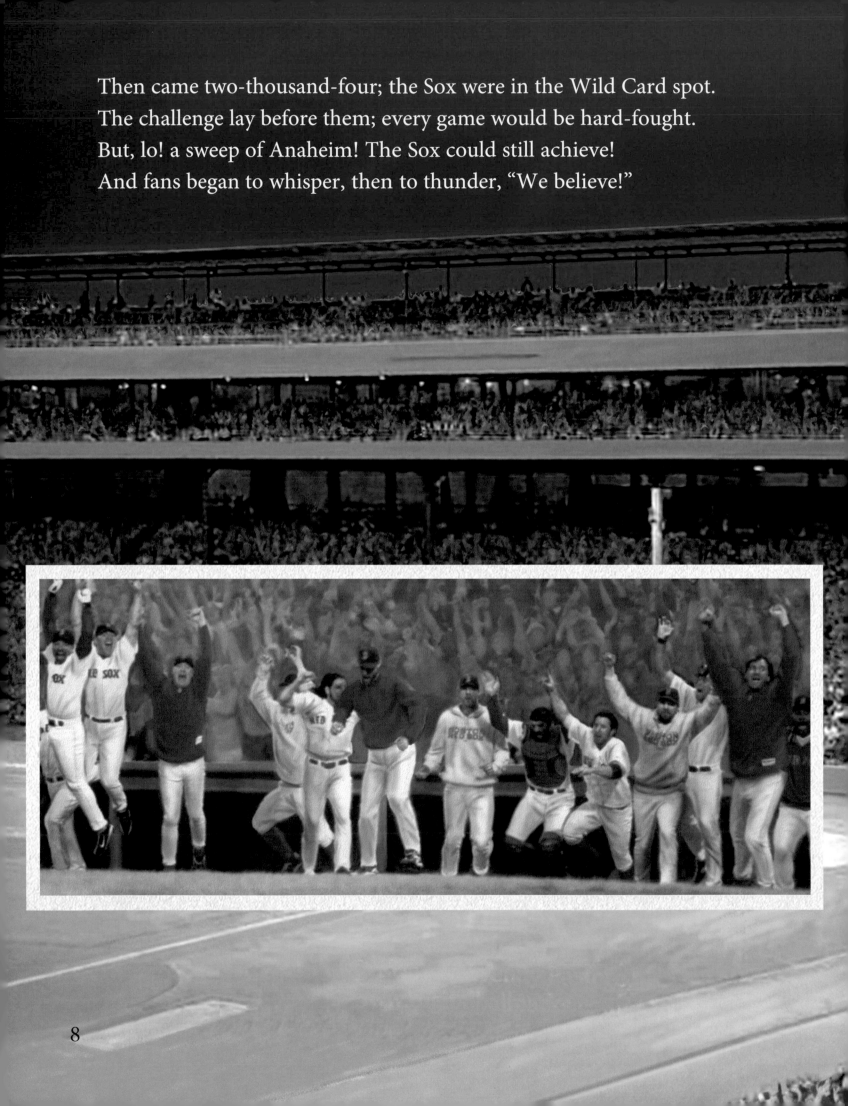

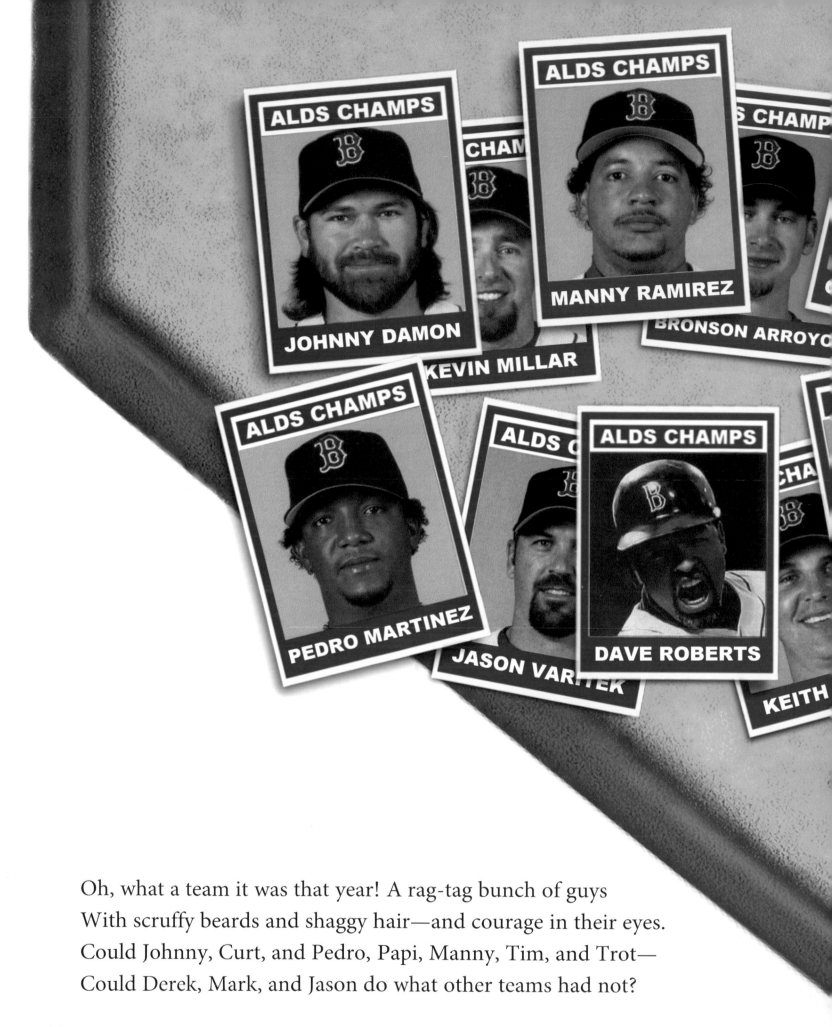

ALDS CHAMPS
JOHNNY DAMON

ALDS CHAMPS
MANNY RAMIREZ

CHAM

KEVIN MILLAR

S CHAMP

BRONSON ARROYO

ALDS CHAMPS
PEDRO MARTINEZ

ALDS C

ALDS CHAMPS
DAVE ROBERTS

JASON VARITEK

CHA

KEITH

Oh, what a team it was that year! A rag-tag bunch of guys
With scruffy beards and shaggy hair—and courage in their eyes.
Could Johnny, Curt, and Pedro, Papi, Manny, Tim, and Trot—
Could Derek, Mark, and Jason do what other teams had not?

ALDS CHAMPS

T SCHILLING

IRABELLI

LL MUELLER

ORLANDO CAB

ALDS CHAMPS

MARK BELLHORN

S CHAMPS

TIM WAK

LKE

ALDS CHAMPS

DAVID ORTIZ

CHAMPS

TROT NIXON

ALDS CHAMPS

DEREK LOWE

Who would they face? The Yankees! for the ALCS crown.
The Sox would do their best to bring the "house that Ruth built" down.
But nothing clicked, night after night; they couldn't blame the ump,
And one, two, three—they lost three games; the Sox were in a slump!

Game Four: the night was chilly as the Red Sox took the field,
The series stood at "oh" and three, but Boston did not yield.
Three outs and it would all be lost—then Roberts stole a base!
Through inning twelve they persevered: the Sox stayed in the race!

Each night the same; they HAD to win, their backs against the wall;
And Red Sox Nation held its breath for every "Strike" and "Ball."

14

Game Five stretched on into the night, the fourteenth inning came;
At last, on Papi's single, Damon scored to win the game!

And so, Game Six, back in New York—the Red Sox turned to Curt.
He'd faltered in his first time out, his right foot badly hurt.
The pitching would decide the game, as Schilling took the mound,
His ankle held with stitches and with bandage tightly wound—

For seven brilliant innings, Schilling pitched through stabbing pain.
He knew the Sox had much to lose—and everything to gain.
Curt's courage made the difference; Bellhorn's homer made the score;
The Red Sox had accomplished what no team had done before!

The Daily Times

RED SOX FORCE GAME SEVEN

First Time in History

The time had come to face the past and drive away Babe's ghost.
Sox fans could barely dare to dream of what they wanted most!
No curse of eighty-six long years would make their spirits fade;
Game Seven was the crossroads: time for hist'ry to be made.

First inning: Papi gripped the bat and saw the ball in flight,
Then slugged it with a mighty crack and sailed it out of sight.
A home run! And the crowd grew still—the Yankee fans were sore,
But back in Boston, Red Sox Nation echoed with a roar!

19

A roar that grew and grew as that momentous night wore on.
The Red Sox won it, ten to three! Was Babe's ghost really gone?
A comeback for the ages! and a vict'ry, oh, so sweet!
But the story wasn't over; there was destiny to meet . . .

The Series! The World Series was the prize they had to take!
To end the curse that, through the years, caused Boston's heart to break.
Three generations' loyalty had been put to the test.
Could this year be the one that would make up for all the rest?

Father and me 1918.

St. Louis was the team to beat, back home at Fenway Park.
Game One of the World Series on a night cold, damp, and dark:
Though Sox fans had to clutch their hearts with every Card'nal run,
What mattered was the outcome, and the Red Sox had Game One.

Curt Schilling proved his fortitude with every pitch he threw,
And Embree, Foulke, and Timlin finished up to take Game Two.
Game Three moved to St. Louis; Pedro had his chance to soar.
He owned the game; the Sox prevailed. The next step was Game Four . . .

Was Babe's curse really over? Were they just one game away?
The fans were tired and nervous all 'round Boston on that day,
October twenty-seventh; for ten days they'd had no sleep.
They thought they might be dreaming—could there really be a sweep?

Oh, somewhere men are sighing or they're dabbing at a tear,
And moms are tucking in their kids with, "Wait until next year."
And somewhere fans are mournful as October shadows fall,

But they're filled with joy in Boston,

'CAUSE THE RED SOX WON IT ALL!

2004 World Champion
BOSTON RED SOX

Terry Adams	53	Pitcher
Bronson Arroyo	61	Pitcher
Mark Bellhorn	12	Second Base
Orlando Cabrera	44	Shortstop
Johnny Damon	18	Outfield
Lenny DiNardo	55	Pitcher
Alan Embree	43	Pitcher
Keith Foulke	29	Pitcher
Terry Francona	47	Manager
Gabe Kapler	19	Outfield
Curtis Leskanic	30	Pitcher
Derek Lowe	32	Pitcher
Pedro Martinez	45	Pitcher
David McCarty	10	First Base
Ramiro Mendoza	26	Pitcher
Doug Mientkiewicz	13	First Base
Kevin Millar	15	First Base
Doug Mirabelli	28	Catcher
Bill Mueller	11	Third Base
Mike Myers	36	Pitcher
Trot Nixon	7	Outfield
David "Papi" Ortiz	34	Designated Hitter
Manny Ramirez	24	Outfield
Pokey Reese	3	Second Base
Dave Roberts	31	Outfield
Curt Schilling	38	Pitcher
Mike Timlin	50	Pitcher
Jason Varitek	33	Catcher
Tim Wakefield	49	Pitcher
Scott Williamson	48	Pitcher
Kevin Youkilis	20	Third Base